Vineyard Passages

Text and photography by

CHEEVER TYLER

Published by
Douglas Charles Press
7 Adamsdale Road
North Attleborough
MA 02760

ISBN 1-58066-022-3

Edited by Nancy Moore Brochin
Designed by Liisa Lindholm
Set in Adobe Garamond and printed in Korea

Preface

Proceeds from the sale of this book will be given
to the Permanent Endowment for Martha's Vineyard
in appreciation for the value a community foundation
can give to its neighbors, and to encourage others
to do likewise.

HIGH COLOR – EDGARTOWN

A harmony
intensifies the suspicion
that there may never be
a time as good as this.
In the cool afternoon light,
comfortable shoes
reveal their importance
to the immersing island watercolor.
Within this light,
the right to create art,
and the sweet smell of wisteria;
aware of your weakness,
time slows to infinity.

DISCUSSING MARKETING ON THE CHAPPY ROAD

The screen door slams
a punctuation sign
as the shingles' graying
keeps on in the quiet.
Beach and beast are hot to the touch.
Bathing suits cling like
second skins to little kids
playing in the shade
in sandy sweat.
Even the finches fly up
then dive, not flapping,
in slow half circles,
cooling themselves off,
yellow against a yellow sky.
A ceiling fan turns indifferently
against the thick air.
There is nothing to do but
look at you
next to me on the porch
sipping your lemonade.
You are happy to be here,
and I'm happy you are,
even though it's sticky.

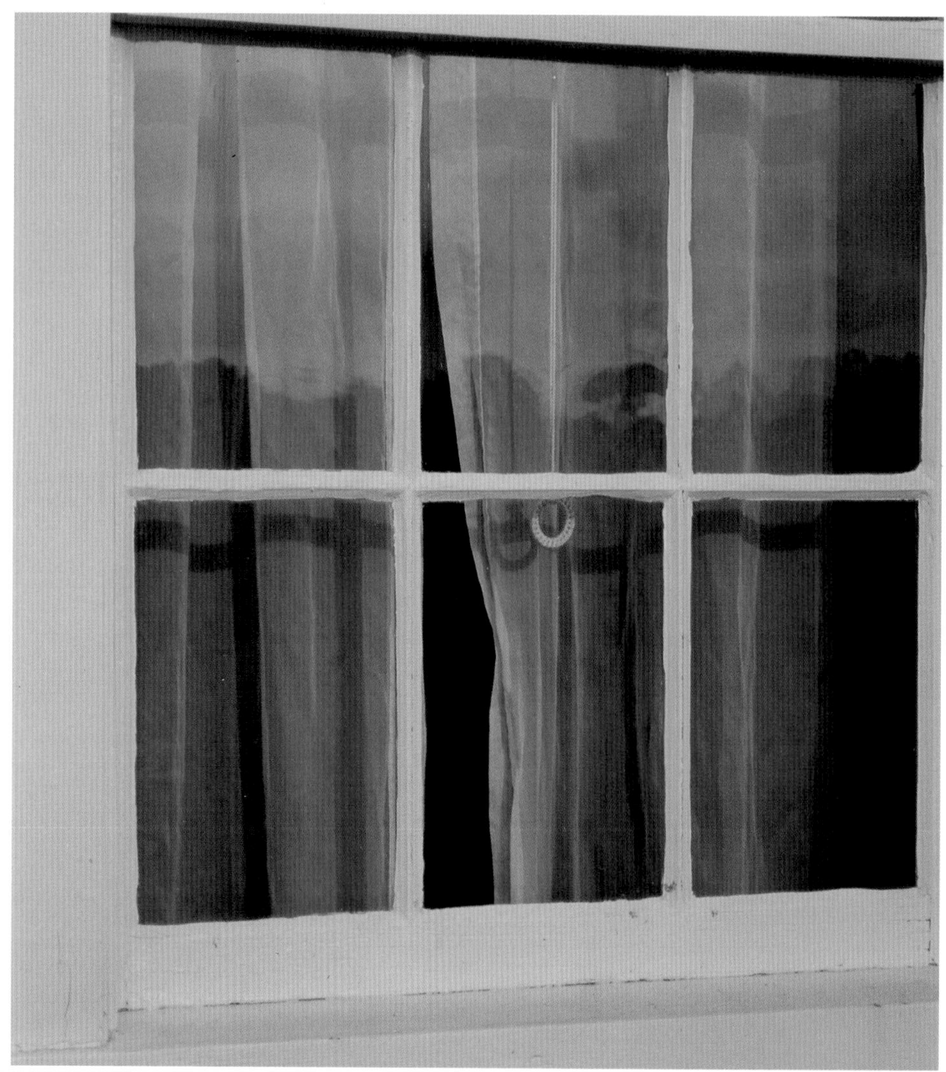

WINDOW ON YESTERDAY – TOM'S NECK FARM

Black Jack

Our black lab, Jack,
lies darkly under the deck
looking out at the heat
that has brought me
onto the screened porch
where I curl,
sipping iced tea.
The mosquitoes are thick,
but we don't care.
We aren't waiting
for anything,
are we Jack?

THE LOST BARN – TOM'S NECK FARM

New Paint

The first light plays
the small window panes
on the new paint. In the
hand finished room,
the strike marks of the
old farmer's axe
from the days of oxen,
seem fresher than in the gray
barn across the road.
Beyond the morning frost
on the old window,
the hard, corded wood
carefully cut and stacked
in the anticipation
that comes before the cycle of seasons,
waits to be summoned inside,
like the sleek black dogs called in,
eager, from the fields.

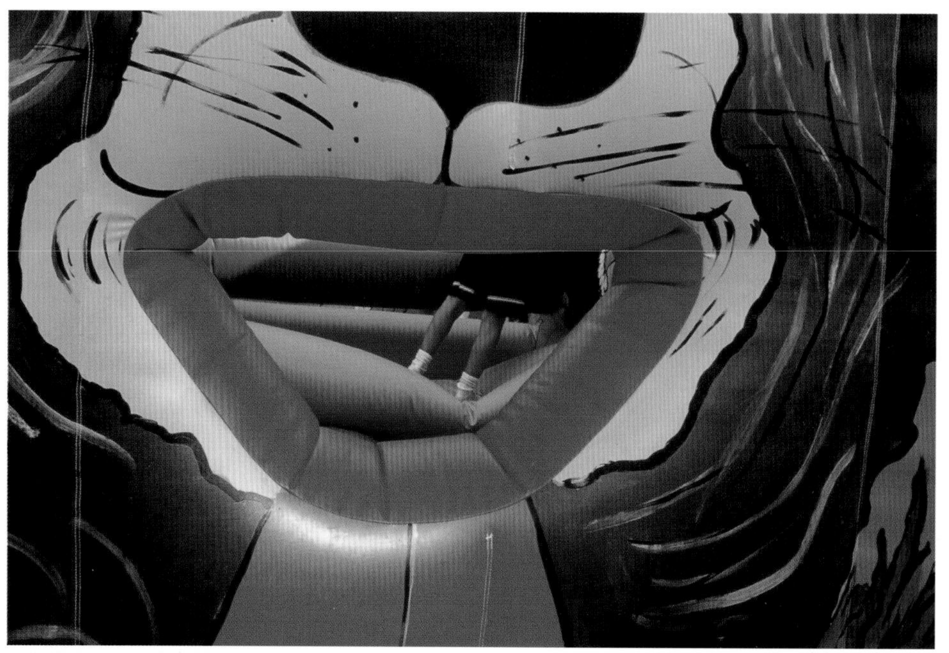

CHILDREN AT THE TISBURY FAIR

Three

Do you suppose it matters
that you are three and I am thirty?
All I can imagine is that
I must hold your hand crossing streets
and pick you up when you cry.
But, when you are a woman,
you will drive me in your car,
and nothing will have changed, but
you will be bigger,
and I will be smaller.

GIRLS ON EAST BEACH

Blue Boys

The first cool gust of air, then
reds, then yellows
pass by softly underfoot.
Sails, folded into stuffed bags rest
like fat blue boys side by side
full enough of summer.
Come, the path leads to the bay
where smells of wood smoke
remind us that the great room will be
warm on our return. Come,
and I will show you that
warmth is everywhere
in the October time of this afternoon,
and that there is grace
in growing old.

WEDNESDAY AT THE TABERNACLE

Soft rain on the deck furniture;
rain bowing the heads
of gentle impatiens;
rain darkening the bollards
of the town dock,
warming the tranquil bay.
Rain bowing the head
of summer's gaiety, so unaware,
just yesterday,
that one of its colors might be gray.
Inside, at the eight o'clock service,
in the white of communion,
I hear the whispers
of the unsinning
confessing their sins, hoping,
while the soft rain falls and falls,
bowing their heads, too.

SUMMER MOVIES

Blue Eyes

Gray rocks, gray fog, harbor,
piers, roofs, gray, gray
houses, barns.
Roses white fences,
green arbors, and blue eyes.
What then are the consequences
of wanting what you can't have?

HAVEN AND THE OLD CARRIAGE

Standing in cool water
over my knees
I feel the little blue boat
tug at its string,
anxious to run off
across Cape Pogue
after a red boat
full of kids.
We both know
it is time to
absorb the late afternoon,
golden in the lowering day
full of ospreys and terns
fishing,
and to wonder
at the painter's way
with pastels.

ILLUMINATION NIGHT – OAK BLUFFS

Old Mirror

Clear blue, the old mirror
like a smoky street light
in deep Atlantis
makes its silent way
into the night,
showing things chalky soft.
On the sea, the old mirror
leaves a silver path, pointing to
the high, cold, dusty source
of ancient myth and wonder.
Its stillness makes us still.
Out in the summer garden,
the light touches your face,
and you feel the
delicate, silent,
ageless contact
that now, from a great distance,
reflects you too.

NAT AT TOM'S NECK

Distant Boy

My island has given me time
to be alone with it in October.
The watery reach of the foaming ebb,
ends at my feet, washing
my footprints into sand.
The vastness is too great
for me to understand in my way,
but I know I will be given no other.
Perhaps it is not for me to see;
perhaps there is someone
watching; perhaps it is all
within a glass enclosure
into which a small boy, far distant,
may be looking, watching,
amused by a man walking on a beach
listening for his voice.

RAIN ON THE "ON TIME"

Nobska

The old ferry glides
toward Vineyard Haven
before my closing eyes, as
memories of my children
stand waving on the dock.
As I think of her, I know that
time has touched her, much as
time will wear in a baseball glove, or
soften the wooden handle
of a pen knife in a boy's pocket
smoothing old Nobska
in my dark inner theater
as though she were
a great rock in a deep, cold stream.
Water rushes past her,
emerging from a state of being
that has no beginning and no end.
I imagine her now, returning
from an old acquaintance,
where, inside my thoughts,
having had no beginning,
she will have no end.

FRITZ AND COLIN ON WASQUE

Fritz

Reverence and irreverence blend
in the old oaken cask
where we go to dip our cups
when our souls are dry.
I like to watch you
stir the mix, old Fritz,
so we can laugh
about the paradox
that makes it possible
for us to understand.

QUIET TIME – CHILMARK

Rain Sound

The storm came and
touched us in the night,
leaving, snarling
for another appointment.
In the morning,
we lie in a warm bed,
and nothing matters
but the
sound of rain.

SAYING GOODBYE – VINEYARD HAVEN

Give me the dream catcher's song
to prolong my immersion
in the light
that comes from the sea around
five in the afternoon,
after a soft air day.
Give me a song,
because light travels
at the speed of light, and
only a dream catcher
can keep it, so that
its thousand instants
can become less than time,
slowing, slowing,
never to forget.

GETTING CLOSER – OAK BLUFFS

Carnival Ride

Katama, still as stainless steel,
reflects the lowering sun
until a wind ruffles it,
and the revolving earth
absorbs the golden ball
soundlessly into its soft pocket.
Even the birds become still
when they see
that they too are on a
great carnival ride.
Thrown off balance,
they sit in trees, holding on.
In the golden finale,
we watch them.
Can they hear
a carousel's music,
or feel a slowing hand?
How many, they seem to wonder,
how many spins after this,
will there be?

GRAIN AND FEED – TISBURY

Be Well

The great horses
pulling their enormous weights,
and dogs herding sheep,
both knowing the game;
cotton candy and
rubber lizards on sticks
reappear in August at the Old Fair
to put a mark on summer,
much as buoys along the coast
reassure us that someone
wants us to be well.

HORSES LOOSE IN OAK BLUFFS

Hold on Tight

Heraldic, flaring steeds,
pawing within
a circular gentility,
bearing Sir Hold On Tight,
and Sir One More Time,
voyage out into distant glades
to tilt with the evil baron, Brass Rings.
The mighty chargers
stop now and then
to gather up other little knights
who ride fiercely away, and,
having won the field,
always come home again
to me.

THE NEXT GENERATION ON TOM'S NECK

Knees

Isn't it peculiar that
we come
in different shapes, elbows,
heights, colors, weights,
wrinkle patterns,
baldness patterns,
ear sizes, eye colors, knees,
teeth, dispositions,
predilections, fears
and the capacity to love
and grip with our thumbs,
all of which leads us to
the conclusion that we are
different from one another,
when, it certainly seems, we
are not?

BILLY'S HORSE – OAK BLUFFS

That Old Familiar Tune

Listen to the distant horn
on the sea, the morning
dove's cool oboe,
the trumpet of gulls
skimming under the fog,
and the soft timpani
of rain closing us inward
into a place we cannot see
but know well.
Come, be still for a moment,
so the hands
holding around the
gathering table
can hear that old, familiar tune.

MEMORIAL DAY, EDGARTOWN

Old Soldier

Early on a cool fall morning,
I passed by the cemetery
where, beyond a white picket fence,
rows of uneven stone panels
stood like weary old soldiers
risen stoically from their fall.
Nearby, on a faded wooden bench,
an old man slept,
fetal in the morning light,
his hands hiding his eyes
from the sight beyond his swollen fingers, while
the newspapers that had
shielded him in the night, lay strewn
around his slumber.
Here lay an old man
once a child, once a youth, once
a father perchance, a son,
but for now, an old soldier
not yet risen from his fall.

EDWINA AND CORY, EDITING

Being an editor isn't as easy
as some people think.
In this case, it was
love at first sight.
We talked about whether
the period at the end of
a sentence
should go inside or
outside of
quotation marks.
I went to get a text,
and when I came back,
she was gone,
a beautiful summer
romance done in
by punctuation.

A SAND RIVER ON CHAPPAQUIDDICK

The white house with its barns
announce the farm,
whose stone walls and
trodden paths have carved
the pastures and fields
where the unambiguous
canvases of summer and winter
have been painted.
Within, the pictures of Mary
and her family
have touched the old wood,
and smoothed it like rocks
in the brook, over which clear, honest
water has gone down from here
to the Great Missouri,
and in its cradle, out to sea.
Behind, in the white house,
the banister on the curving stair
awaits the touch
of little children's hands,
climbing up to bed.

FOURTH OF JULY – EDGARTOWN

There are only a few of us
on the ferry Schamonshi,
alone, deep within our own
imagined destinations;
solitary, thinking out
across the morning calm
like ghosts in October
mocking the end
of a summer civilization,
where voyagers with hats,
once eager in these rows
of empty blue benches,
have gone.

GIRL WITH TATTOO GOING HOME

Long ago rolled up
by the cold Atlantic,
the ancient stone
held in your hand
that last day in October,
weighs lightly on my fingers.
Discovered in the pocket
of faded summer clothing,
your warmth, long held within
the Ancient Messenger, returns.
Soon, I will look for you
in other places,
for awhile.

BEAUTY IN THE PARADE – EDGARTOWN

Beer Truck

The Vineyard Haven band
leading the Fourth of July Parade has just gone by
in a farm truck, in which a black lab
with a long pink tongue
also lies, panting and observant.
There's Larry in his fifty-three-year-old khakis,
an old soldier full of memories,
stepping high to a cadence from long ago.
Then comes Bob from the A&P,
who lost his leg in Viet Nam,
and Ted, the sometime real estate lawyer
whose big job is with the volunteer fire fighters.
The beer truck
has a large nearly naked man
in a grass skirt
and beer can brassiere riding the hood.
A sign on the back of the truck says "Eat Me!"
A bus full of sweet old ladies
singing Christmas carols
floats by on this day of celebration
in which we all wrap ourselves
in the flag and get to show off
some little things, and some very big things
in our lives.

GOSPEL SONG – OAK BLUFFS

An egret, bursting out of the harbor,
skims across the morning calm,
its wings like the drumbeats of reveille
tap the water
in strong measure
before its flight becomes silent.
Across the bay, the early raised flags
flap away from the wind,
while boats at anchor
turn into it, anxious
to be free.
Church spires, bright in
the morning light, rise
above clapboard faces
ringing the harbor.
Just down Fair Street,
they sing "Abide in Me"
as May Ellen plays the organ, and
the old parishioners say the Lord's Prayer.
Breathe deep, sister.
There is precision in this
that could not have happened
by chance.

LESLIE'S WORLD – CHAPPY

I thought I saw you,
your back to me in the shade,
alone, looking toward Nantucket.
I knew everything of you,
but not this.
You turned your head
in the old way.
You stood on one foot,
the other behind
in the old way.
Your hands held a book
as they had held mine,
in the old way.
My heart beating said
"Why have you come?"
and you turned and
looked at me
in the old way.

HAVEN ON THE CAPTAIN'S WALK

Until you start a thirty minute trip
with twenty eight minutes
to do it in, you're not sure that
prayer is good for you.
It's an open and shut case.
There's no getting around it.
But, I wasn't so sure until
we were late for the ferry.
Someone has lost a hairband,
and don't worry, there's time.
Tick and tock are real. They exist.
The truth is that
I am a far better person
for having given up all those
bad habits in return for
the ferry being delayed
just long enough.
It's a certain thing.
Prayer is good for you.
You can take that to the bank.

FOGGY DAY ON WASQUE

Footprints along the autumn pond's edge
lead to you. The curling ocean
probing the barrier beach, and
tall grasses, waiting, still, in the cool of morning,
hear me say "My father said
good luck follows skipping stones."
So, full of a boy's hope,
I skip you my stone,
barely touching the reflecting steel
until it falls off the edge, exhausted.
After a while, I turn,
gray, and much older now, and watch
the long trail of footprints in the sand,
as they follow you away.

SANDCASTLES ON CHAPPY

ILLUMINATION NIGHT – OAK BLUFFS

Bright colors, gay, asking for attention
as if to counterbalance carvings,
define the little house in Oak Bluffs.
Inside, through the screens, are simple
people who may be from upstate New York,
and who may be called Frank and Ada.
Practical, straightforward, honest they
attend at church, use respectful
language, and have well formed handwriting.
It all restates a time when it was good
to be the way Norman Rockwell
painted the American people, and
peaceful afternoons were broken by
news from the war front, heard,
as from a great distance,
on a wooden radio in the parlor.
Two blocks away, heavy, sweaty men with
long hair, sleeveless leather, Wermacht helmets
and large tattoos, ride growling
black Harleys up Circuit Avenue
while Ada and Frank,
moving quietly about their house,
put out flypaper.

HOLD THE HOME FRIES – EDGARTOWN

I had a cheese omelette this morning
at the Edgartown Deli.
What's best about being alone
at times like this
is not having to say
"I usually don't!"

WALKER AT THE WHALING CHURCH – EDGARTOWN

A miniature man,
maybe three, maybe four,
is very declarative
as he points out things
he knows
to his young mother
as they walk
along Summer Street.
It occurs to me
to listen,
because he
has seen the Teacher
more recently
than I.

MORNING

The Early Bell

The clarity of the dawn,
summons the early
bell from the village;
the air, strong
as ice, descends, deep.
From a high place, I summon
Nantucket, precise
and available,
still tethered
to this vast ocean ship.
The chill, fall air is unambiguous,
leaving no doubt behind,
as the warming wind
picks up from the Northeast,
and the stirring island
gets down to business.

COLIN AND PHIL AT SUNSET – CHAPPY

Playing Catch

They were kids with me,
so I like watching those two
gray, woolly guys laugh,
reaching down into their wisdom
to bring up sparklers
to show the other
who's just been there himself.
How kind, how bright,
how tough in little things,
they know when something
is funny, and pounce on it
merrily, tossing it back
and forth, playing catch, until it has
lost its energy, the sound
of discovery resonant,
not tired. Heads smoothed to gray
by time's running fluid,
two woolly guys
sitting on my deck by the sea
at day's end, warm, like
beach stones in your hand.

LARRY AT THE TOP OF HIS GAME

Larry

Larry's aggressive for a liberal Democrat,
an elephant hunter of the old school,
waiting eagerly
for some furry conservative nuance
or feathery Republican inconsistency
to come along in the forest.
And, when he shows what he's bagged,
his laugh, like the crackle of musketry,
fills up with the delight
of chase and capture.
It's pleasant to watch him work,
prowling stealthily through newspapers,
with his bright magnifying glass,
looking at everything.

LIFEGUARD STATION ON WASQUE BEACH

The wind in the pines
like a vast engine gunning
through the morning,
bends the forest to the marsh.
Across ruffled Katama,
the real stuff is angry,
pounding Wasque beach,
ripping at the barrier.
Old dog stays
near me, not wagging.
Everything is tense,
waiting for the wind borne
soldiers to invade.

The Standby Line

What can be said for the Standby Line?
It's always too long,
but, on the other hand,
it is always full of dogs.

All Wet

Walking in the rain
is better than
standing in it, but
standing in the
outdoor shower
is better yet.

The great silver bass
lies at last still
on the night beach,
staring at a fixed point,
perhaps a star.
The monument is revealed
in all the glory of
its secret, watery life,
undiminished by the
struggle it may have lost,
but the star gazer may have won.

SAM JACKSON ON CHAPPY

Mr. White

Pasture green, rising to the line of oak,
shaded where the white horse stands.
Where can the movement be that evolves
dust to dust, but rebirth in each sense
we share in this pasture?
What vision do we lack, Mr. White,
to see the truth that is just beyond?
Perhaps, in the stillness,
we have come to the edge of knowing,
you and I, here, by the old stone wall.

SALLY AND PHIL ON WASQUE

Faded Blue Shirt

I go there to find things
that must be left behind,
for they don't travel well.
The album of these images
has no size or shape, but
in time, its store of me
fits like the faded blue shirt
left there in the closet.
My pile is carefully
arranged so visits can be casual.
Yet tonight, turning the pages again,
there is nothing offhand
about what is there.

Ann's Farm

Afternoon colors of fall in the fields,
dry yellow grass rising through
the rusted plow, long beyond tilling;
and gray shingles, hanging tired, tired.
Ann, in the window
through her grandmother's curtains
looks at the barn,
decayed forever
in the memory
of harvest.

The Harmonica

The night fog
had subdued Menemsha, pushing down.
Voices that should have been whispers
hushed by lights no longer helpful, had no echo;
the water black, hard and waiting.
Growling boats that had killed big fish,
were leashed
with thundering engines still,
on Dutcher dock.
An emerging window
in a large, corpulent yacht,
revealed a large, corpulent,
nearly naked man sitting in a wicker chair,
his arms hanging down like
the thick stalks of a white wisteria.
Down the dock,
the smell of a fishing life, and a young man,
whose boat had been to the Canyon,
played a harmonica,
while an older man
cut apart the carcasses
of the sea.

DAVID RYAN'S – EDGARTOWN

A ninety-seven-year-old woman
comes to the podium and,
taking the microphone,
tells the crowd in the Tabernacle
what it was like
when she was a girl.
What it was like in those days
when people would hang
Japanese lanterns on their houses
and sing songs about America
and the goodness of the earth,
just as we do tonight.
The crowd cheers, and all over the square
lanterns blossom into light.
You could sing from end to end.
How about a dance, sweetheart?
It's time we were steppin' out.

BLUES ON WASQUE

Out from the struggling, foamy end
to the surge of surf, footprints
mark the casting arc.
The small splash takes place
in the rip's current
rushing by Wasque.
It is a delicate beginning,
yet, when my lure's deception
calls the struggling hunter
to enter air and show
his colors on the sand,
what was clear is no longer clear.
What was simple is
no longer simple.

MOPEDS – EVERYWHERE

As if by seasonal migration, we lemming
off to the edge of the ocean to get sand in
our bathing suits, sandals, and sandwiches.
My cousin Harvey puts baby oil on himself,
and when he is finished, he
looks like a cue ball in a Caesar salad.
Wait till he gets sand on himself, I think.
The beach umbrella is rusted shut, and we
forgot the Frisbee. But floating beyond
the curlers, watching, I like it so much, you know,
I wish I could have a cigar.

PIERCE ON EAST BEACH – CHAPPAQUIDDICK

Oars

It's the evening light
on my father's oars
that retrieves him from a time
when he came with them
to this island,
a time when he,
one autumn, perhaps,
may have seen an evening light
such as this, in dark eyes.
The graceful sweeps are
on the wall, far from
his grip and pull.
Now, it's day's end, my old friend.
And, I'm looking at your oars,
thinking of you rowing, bending to it.
Nothing's ahead
for you, now, but music
and dark eyes.

AN OLD TWELVE METER – EDGARTOWN HARBOR

The hard blue edge,
taut, men under
snapping canvas, jibe
the big boat out of the harbor,
turning on graceful lines,
reined like a great stallion
by ropes running
on holystoned decks.
The regatta begins, strained wood
creaks as eyes are keen
to trim and balance.
Listen, and you can hear the voices
of the lifting, carved water,
and of strong men, playing
their stately instrument
on the sea.

THE FIRST COOL GUST OF AIR – CHAPPY

Zig Zag

Through tall windows,
the great oak's inner source, green,
touching the airy yellows
of twilight, peers into
the Old Whaling Church, inquisitive
of people listening
to a speaker recalling
the history of women's rights.
A small choir of girls sings "America" as
people cool themselves with fans on sticks.
Outside, a brown dog curls
against the white clapboard, waiting,
while a blond boy, bent on some errand,
hurries by on his bicycle,
zigs, and is gone.
The only sound,
the sound of clapping from within,
seems appropriate.

EMBLEMS – EDGARTOWN

The soft air
blowing through the
church's open windows,
beckons the soaring voices
of the congregation
out into Sunday morning
in Oak Bluffs,
where they flow
through joyful gardens,
past wide verandahs
where people talk quietly,
then inside small, dark rooms
where they become still
until the soft air
calls them out again.

CHOICES – CHAPPY

The Old Machine

Art is not an abstraction
on the deck overlooking
Katama Bay.
In the soft sea air,
there is an inner space
in which limitless
possibilities exist, where
his inquiring eyes shape
the concept, testing
for possibilities,
watching the harmonies
until he knows it's time for
his strong hands
to attach wood to steel
and wire to hold glass,
polishing coils
long abandoned
into dramatic reunions
that transcend
the usefulness
of the old machine.

SOMETHING FOR EVERYONE – OAK BLUFFS

I remembered the path to
our old house, still small
in the morning mist.
A new door, curtains, and the
impatiens replaced by yellow,
is no disguise for the place
where our hands
had smoothed the daybreak when,
like an arching lily,
you would blossom to your music.
I have been far from
our room with its
lace curtains floating
near the dark oaken dresser
where you left your summer hat
carelessly, for that last day.
A dove calls near the old clapboard place,
unmistakable, perfect and precise.
It was so very long ago, but I can still hear
a cello playing far away.

THE OLD BIPLANE – EDGARTOWN

Good Smoke

I read his tombstone in the *Gazette*:

Angus MacKenzie, 79

Longtime Vineyard Resident

There was a great deal more to tell and say, but knowing him, I don't suppose he would have cared in the end. But, I want you to hear his story for reasons that have to do with him and with me.

A beginning would be to say that on Chappaquiddick, I'm known as a "summer person." Understand, we aren't migrants. We're more, well, like salmon that come back upstream every summer. They say that unless you spend winters on the island, you'll always be a summer person. Makes sense, I guess. But, there are advantages. Summer people can't vote or run for office, so we're not responsible for anything.

It may surprise you to know that summer people do get to know island people pretty well now and then, like I got to know Angus MacKenzie. It was fishing that started it with us. Somehow fascinated by him, and although he took no notice of me, I made it a habit to stand next to that angular old buzzard on Wasque, casting for blues, watching his shock of white hair blow in the wind, and his incredible arching casts. He belonged there. It was as though he had come from the sea to be on that long, sloping beach. We finally exchanged a few words back up at the rusty red Ford pickup he had driven to the spot by the rip. Angus was out of cigarettes, so I gave him a good cigar, which made him smile. It was a smile I doubt many other summer people had ever seen.
"My name's Tom," I said.
"Mine's Angus." We didn't shake.

There was a long pause in which Angus examined the cigar, took it admiringly from its glass cylinder, smelled its entire length, slipped the empty container into his shirt pocket which was barely visible over his chest-high waders, bit off the end, spit it out and lit the cigar. The light from the match illuminated his sharp, craggy face. He drew on the cigar, dwarfed in his massive, powerful hands, and nodded appreciatively.

"When I die, I want to be back in Scotland, and I'd like to be smokin' a cigar like this when I go."
"I've got another one here, if you're not feeling too good," I replied, rewarded with another grin.
He drew on the cigar again, slowly.
"That's a nice sunset, I'd like to be up in it," he said casually. But, there was no masking the tinge of longing in his voice.
"How so?" There was a long pause.
"I'm a flier," he said, making me think that he had regretted exposing that much.
"Me too," I said.
My statement penetrated and then embedded itself. It seemed it was time to open the door some, so I told him I had been a Navy pilot, which made him smile again.
"I flew Spitfires." There was another long pause as Angus drew on the cigar. "Got eight."
I knew that eight kills would make Angus an ace, which was something every fighter pilot dreamed of. But I wondered fleetingly if there was a "touch of the poet" as they say, behind the deep, weathered eyes. A story for summer people.
I dismissed it when he said, "You ought to come flyin' with me."
Angus was an easy seventy-five or more, and still an active pilot. There was no way to fake that.
"Got a Stearman," he said confidently. "Take people for rides."
"Over at Katama?" I asked.
"Yep."
I had seen the graceful old biplane making slow circles over Katama Bay in summer afternoons.
"How come you're not flying tonight, then?" I asked.
"Superstition. Never fly near dark." It was his call. I left it at that.

When the sun had set, we stopped fishing. Angus had two large blues, and he put them into the bed of his truck, along with his rod. He held up the stub of the cigar. "Good smoke," he said, and rattled off down the beach.

In the days that followed, Angus and I fished together occasionally. He talked with me about the war, and about his wife who had died with their infant son in the bombing of London. He talked about his anger, and how he was taught to defeat the German pilots, using the Spitfire's superior flying characteristics. I saw a tattered photograph of him in his RAF uniform, handsome as a Scottish king. I told him about my family and my law practice. I wanted him to meet Sally, but he declined. "I'm not good at such things," was the message. It had finality to it.

So, we would be friends his way. We talked about flying, but he didn't mention the Stearman again. I think he was afraid I would ask to pay for the ride, like one of his customers, and that would have embarrassed him. I would wait for him to bring it up. Sure enough, one day, on the beach, he put up his pole and walked over to me.

"How about tomorrow at three?" he asked.

The plane was tethered at the grass field at Katama. It was larger than I had remembered Stearmans to be, and it seemed prehistoric compared to the trim Cessna sitting lightly beside it. Angus' hands touched the bird with an incredible delicacy, and with a sureness only a good pilot would have. He inspected the canvas-covered machine like a pediatrician examining a baby, knowing what to look for, but not probing.

The noise in the front seat was deafening. I made no effort to handle the controls, and Angus offered me none. The smell of aviation gas and oil was like it must have been in the days of dogfights between gentlemen flying Gypsy Moths and Fokkers over France. His one concession to modern technology, a helmet with a microphone and earphones, made it possible for me and Angus to speak, which we barely did, both because Angus wasn't a talker and because the roar of the massive radial engine and the broad-bladed wooden propeller was impenetrable.

There was a deep thunder from the engine as the Stearman ran down the grass field, lifting into the air long before I would have asked it to. I noticed the stick. It had barely moved. We flew to Angus' accustomed grounds over Katama Bay near Wasque.

"See any fish?" I asked. No answer. We flew on.
Then I asked, "How about some aerobatics?"

He was behind me, and I couldn't see his face, but his voice was clear and loud in my earphones. "Don't do aerobatics. Plane's too old."

The ground-awkward bird, now airborne, came alive in Angus' hands. Every turn was natural and full of the grace airplanes can have when they are understood. The landing was silken, as though we had never left the ground. There was no squeak of the tires biting into the grass, just the slowing of the propeller as the tail wheel settled with a slight bump.

Glancing around the cockpit, I could see that Angus had restored all of it. The instruments were polished and active. His touch was everywhere, and the guttural machine seemed to know it.
The airplane came to rest and turned itself off, letting the stout propeller blades spin slower and slower, until it was at rest. We climbed down.
"Thanks," I said.
Angus looked at me and winked. "Next time, you can fly her."

It was, oh, perhaps two years later when I saw him again. Sally and I had been in London and had missed a summer on the island. In the following spring, I called Angus and asked if he would fish with me.
"Can't," he said.
"Okay, then. How about breakfast at seven thirty tomorrow at the Edgartown deli?"
There was a pause. "Okay Tom. I'll see ya there." I was puzzled because he rarely, if ever used my name.

In the morning, he was there, looking distantly through the front window. I saw him before he saw me, and I knew from everything about him that he was being eaten alive from within. I sat down, and he nodded.
"What's wrong, Angus? " I asked.
He looked at me a long time. "Something's got me."
"What is it?" I asked, anxious.
"Can't say," he replied.

"Don't know?"

"No, I don't."

We ate, and I did the talking. He would nod now and then, and I could see his once powerful hands shake on their way to his mouth with breakfast.

"I brought something for you," I said.

He looked up, interested. I took one of his cigars from my pocket and handed it to him. His eyes sparkled and seemed almost to tear, but he looked away before putting the cigar, unopened, into his pocket.

"Thanks," he said.

"How's the plane?" I offered.

"Pretty," he said, smiling.

That evening, the air was cool and crisp. I was on the deck as the sunset gathered for its glory like an orchestra tuning. The grays, the blues, and the orange-gold clouds reflected on the bay so that the water became a part of the sky, the clouds stark against the darkening day. Birds stopped flying and sat in trees, watching the splendor of day's end. Stillness was thick in the air.

Then I heard it. The distant sound of the radial engine pulling the graceful Stearman over the bay. As I watched, the plane climbed on its tail, high, then arced on its back in a long slow dive, twisting at the end over the water. Then it was up again, this time into a cloud then racing back down through the golden air. Over and over he looped and swept, guiding the old airplane with loving hands in slow, deliberate but graceful movements.

"Angus," I whispered.

Then it stopped. At the end of a long, diving salute, Angus leveled the old Stearman and flew slowly and majestically out to sea, southeast of Nantucket.

He was on his way to Scotland.

THE OLD GARDEN – EDGARTOWN

Emma Donaldson left her mark on me in many ways. Although, in view of what I have just told you, it would be easy to conclude that we saw a good deal of one another. We did not. She was not reclusive, but her privacy was important. I have learned that islands teach self-sufficiency, from which a need for privacy inevitably flows. So it was with Emma.

She lived on the Vineyard in a modest old farmhouse next to mine. Her home was probably just as it had been long before. It certainly had that air about it. I had been self-conscious when our builder installed track lighting, a modern kitchen and skylights, painting interior rooms white, and thus converting what I had thought to be a pleasant but ordinary house into our architect's idea of a summer fancy. We had not been willing to make do with what had been left, and, though Emma never mentioned it, our conversion of the old house seemed to be a passageway that needed traversing.

I learned from a man who works at the *Gazette* that her husband, Abbott Donaldson, had brought her to the Vineyard in 1945. They had lived in that house until he was killed in a boating accident in 1952. Emma and Abbott had no children. She continued to live alone.

Emma was tall and bony, with a face betraying her European lineage. She had hands that were capable of a working man's grip. Her eyes were crystal blue, with a surprising depth that could go shallow and become opaque like those of a Vineyard lobsterman, searching for his pots in the flying spray of a rough sea. She wore working clothes, faded carpenter's overalls, as Abbott Donaldson had been a carpenter. On Sunday, she would go to church in one of her print dresses, with her curly white hair, carefree during the week, pulled back and tied with a blue or red ribbon.

Emma's garden, for those of us who saw it in different seasons, revealed a symphonic sense of beauty. It was planted with the discipline of a master musician that permitted it to be frivolous in the spring, jaunty in summer and melancholy in the fall. Emma understood and respected the beauty she created. She seemed not to care if the symphony was heard. It was enough to compose the piece.

She was seventy-five when I first spoke to her at any length. There had been introductions before, but they were perfunctory. As there was only a short fence between our gardens, she could see me struggling with my heavy sacks of peat moss, and my indecision about the future home of the plants Sally and I had brought back from the nursery, unsure both of their names and their actual appearance.

"You're using too much peat," she said, bemused.

"Thank you. I'm new at this," I answered, looking up from my kneeling position in front of a freshly dug hole.

"Peat takes the moisture. Keeps it from the flower if you use too much." I was interested that she had called the lily bulb I was planting a "flower," instead of a "plant."

"I'll show you," she said. And in a moment, she was kneeling beside me. While it takes a careful maneuver for me to change from a standing to a kneeling position, Emma came to her knees effortlessly, not caring that the earth that was shielded from my knees by a boat cushion was hard and rocky against hers. She removed some of the peat I had put in the hole, mixed in some topsoil, and effortlessly planted the lily, leaving a moat around the flower to retain moisture.

"Do that, then water 'em good, and fertilize them in the spring."

She rose to her feet as lightly as she had knelt, rocking back and then up. I rose the hard way, with my hands on my knees for balance and leverage. She turned to the row of bulbs that were still lying on the ground, tied in neat bundles.

"You get these from Wendy in Vineyard Haven?" she asked as she paced in front of them like a general inspecting troops.

"Yes. How did you know?"

"There's things I can tell." She continued her inspection. "These will be yellow, these pink and these orange. You ought to get some things other than lilies."

"Don't lilies bloom all summer?" I asked. I had the impression that we had bought bulbs that would produce flowers during July, August, and September.

"Some do and some don't. I was thinking about cleome, impatiens, shasta daisy, or morning glories. You want some annuals and some perennials. Come on. I'll show ya." The invitation was given in order to be accepted, and I was delighted to oblige. I had admired her garden and was hoping to have one like it, one day.

Her depth of knowledge was immense. She walked me through her gardens. They were tended like a parent would tend a child.

I called her "Mrs. Donaldson" the first chance I had to use her name. "Emma's my name, and you can call me that, if I can call you Tom." I had the impression that it was a gift rarely given.

"All right, Emma, you may call me Tom."

She liked my interest in her garden, which was in fact genuine. She knew I was starting from the bottom and would have to rely upon good advice to make my own gardens bloom. She knelt.

"These are cleomes. They're the tallest of my children, but perhaps the most delicate. And these are lilies. Lilies are children that can take care of themselves." She rose and moved, almost like a dancer, to a lattice. "Here you will see the morning glories when it's their time. They'll bloom all summer. I'll give you a few, so you can enjoy them for yourself." Before I could protest, she had taken a few of the pots in which she was starting her plants and was on her way back to our side of the fence.

"I think they'll look good over here," she said as she approached two of our window boxes. Taking a little peat, she planted them expertly.

"Water these when you get the rest planted. And, you should feed them in about ten days. I want my children to be happy over here!" I made a note of the type of food she had recommended. As she made her way back to her side of the low fence, she stopped and turned, coming back into the yard.

"What do you do?" she asked.

"I'm a lawyer, in New York," I replied. "Why do you ask?"

"You ought to know your neighbors, don't you think?"

"Yes, as I have gotten to know you."

"Do you know about wills?" she asked, tentatively.

"Yes, that's what I do, although you should talk with a Massachusetts lawyer about your will if that's why you're asking. New York lawyers don't know Massachusetts law."

"You look like you know more than you're letting on." A vague smile crossed her lips. I laughed, although it was only to cover the fact that I didn't know how to react. But she had finished her part of the conversation and had turned toward her yard, walking gracefully.

We invited Emma for Thanksgiving dinner that year. Our two daughters were coming for their first Thanksgiving in our new house, and Sally thought we should make a gesture in the hope that Emma would accept. We thought of her alone in her house, and preferred that she be with us if she were willing. The idea occurred to us in New York, so Sally called her from there to extend the invitation.

"Of course we do," I heard Sally say. "Oh, no, our girls have asked for you especially. What? Oh, yes. Sure, come if you can then. No, we won't mind. There'll be more than enough." It had been inconclusive.

We arrived on the Vineyard late on the day before Thanksgiving, with a car full of turkey, stuffing, and warm clothes. We opened the house and drew in the deep breaths that mark the beginning of being on the island and the letting go of the places we had left behind. We were busy unpacking, so it wasn't until much later that I looked across to Emma's house. It was dark. I thought briefly about calling her but, recalling the elements of privacy, I decided not to.

The next day I looked again, but there was no activity. I walked over in the morning, aware of the breeze coming off the sea, but she wasn't there. We were busy cooking and setting the Thanksgiving table with our customary dogeared family decorations of paper turkeys and pilgrims, when Emma's name came up.

"How about a place for Emma?" asked Kate.

"Go ahead. If she doesn't come, we can always take it off, don't you think?" Sally's answer was interrupted by a strong knock on the door, which I promptly opened to find Emma on the stoop. She had a print dress on and no coat, even though it was getting bitterly cold. A bouquet of chrysanthemums from her garden was nestled in her arms. Her hair was tied back with a bright red ribbon, and her eyes were sparkling.

"Am I on time?" she asked. For the first time, I perceived shyness in her voice.

We welcomed her, hoping to warm her up and melt her hesitation away. Closing the door to the cold, Kate finished setting the table, and I offered Emma a glass of wine. Dinner was an hour away, and the smells in the house held us within the moment. I could tell that Emma was happy to be with us, although the reserve was not gone. We showered attention on her, and the girls, not sensitive to her need for privacy, asked questions freely. She insisted on arranging the bouquet in one of the blue ceramic vases we kept in the house. The result was simple artistry.

Working on the dinner, I heard, "I was born in France, and when I was grown, I had a job with a symphony." It was a revelation easily made to a teenage girl and a recent college graduate that would not have been made to me.

"Wow! You played in a symphony?" Kate, our older daughter, was captured.

"Yes. I played in Paris."

"What did you play?" Kate was trying to complete the picture.

"Oh, the cello. I had always loved the cello."

"Do you still play?" Sara was now in the game.

"No, now I only work in the garden."

I came into the room. My curiosity seemed to close the opening door. The girls sensed it, and stopped asking questions. Over dinner, Emma was quiet, and sad in some way. Perhaps she missed Abbott and the Thanksgiving dinners they had enjoyed on this island, where closeness to the sea and remoteness are hospitable to the feelings such moments bring. Perhaps she was thinking back to her own family, years ago in France, long before some interruption had closed the flower of her life. She was touched by being with us. It showed in the color in her face and the depth of her eyes.

Later, when it was over, I walked Emma back to her house. We walked silently. I gave her a coat to warm her shoulders. She returned it when we reached her door.

"Thank you so very much," she said as she turned on a light and withdrew into her space.

I lingered a moment in her yard before turning back to our house. I could see the bright lights of our home, full of activity. Kate and Sara were laughing. I couldn't see Sally, but her presence was there. The fire in the hearth was warming the room, sending a glow out into the night. Emma's house was sparsely lit. One light bulb illuminated the space into which this mysterious and somehow endangered woman had gone.

I wandered toward the long field to the ocean to absorb the brisk air. It was getting cold. I was retracing my steps, Emma on my mind, when I heard the strains of the cello. The sound was clear and pure as the November air that surrounded me, and eloquent, like the memories of her life.

ACKNOWLEDGMENTS

There are many of you who are acknowledged by this work, and you all know who you are. But, a few whose names should be in print because you are the ones who took my idea and made it into something you could hold in your hand and read.

Paul Berendsohn at Atlantic Film Works, who made the prints and the early mockups. Paul knows a good image from a bad one. He was never shy about making those distinctions for me. And, he was often right.

Nancy Moore Brochin, who edited the text, and whose "oohs" and "aahs" were worth working for.

Liisa Lindholm, who designed the book, so that it became elegant.

Colin Smith, a great sculptor who understood what I was trying to say and kept me from saying something else.

All of you whose images are in the work, and who connect me to the Vineyard, each one in a special way.

And especially to *Sally*, *Pierce*, *John*, *Haven*, *Nathan*,*Katherine* and *Sara*, because when I'm with you, I'm home.